MY YELLOW BALL

by DEE LILLEGARD

illustrated by SARAH CHAMBERLAIN

DUTTON CHILDREN'S BOOKS • NEW YORK

Library of Congress Cataloging-in-Publication Data
Lillegard, Dee. My yellow ball / by Dee Lillegard;
illustrated by Sarah Chamberlain. — 1st ed.   p. cm.
Summary: A child's yellow ball is played with by hawks,
coyotes, and other animals, who always return it so that it can
be thrown somewhere else.   ISBN 0-525-45078-5
[1. Balls (Sporting goods) — Fiction.   2. Animals — Fiction.]
I. Chamberlain, Sarah, ill.   II. Title.   PZ7.L6275My
1993   [E] — dc20   92-27003   CIP   AC
Published in the United States 1993 by Dutton Children's Books,
a division of Penguin Books USA Inc.
375 Hudson Street, New York, New York 10014
Designed by Adrian Leichter
Printed in U. S. A.
First edition
1 3 5 7 9 10 8 6 4 2

For Camellia and Marielle...

and Cleo, who gave us the yellow ball

D.L.

For my father

S.C.

One day, I threw my yellow ball so far,

it flew over the treetops, over the town,

and clear over the mountains, where two hawks caught it.

They spread their wings and batted it back and forth over

a cloudy net. *Whack! Whack! Whizz! Whack!*

"No more yellow ball," I said.

Then a *whack* and a miss and my yellow ball fell.

It bounced from one mountain peak to another

and another

and another, until it bounced

all the way back home to me.   Then...

I threw my yellow ball so far,

it went flying across the desert,

where a pack of coyotes scrambled after it.

They kicked it and chased it and kicked it and chased it,

playing coyote soccer. "No more yellow ball," I said.

Then the biggest, strongest coyote gave it such
a big, strong kick,

it rolled and rolled across the desert and kept on rolling

all the way back home to me.   Then...

I threw my yellow ball so far,

it soared to a jungle in a faraway place,

where it landed among some chimpanzees. They decided
to have a baseball game.

They pitched it and hit it and chased it and caught it,

leaping and shouting from tree to tree.

"No more yellow ball," I said. Then a chimp hit it so hard,

it flew clear over the palm trees, out of the jungle,

and all the way

back home to me.

Then...

I threw my yellow ball so far,

it sailed clear over the ocean.

A seal juggled it.

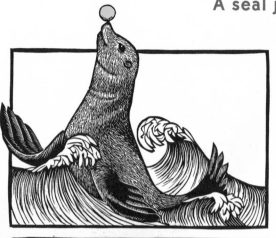

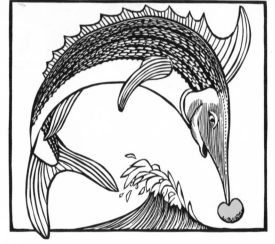

A swordfish poked it. And an octopus played catch with it, all by himself. "No more yellow ball," I said.

Then a tuna gave it a flip with her fin.

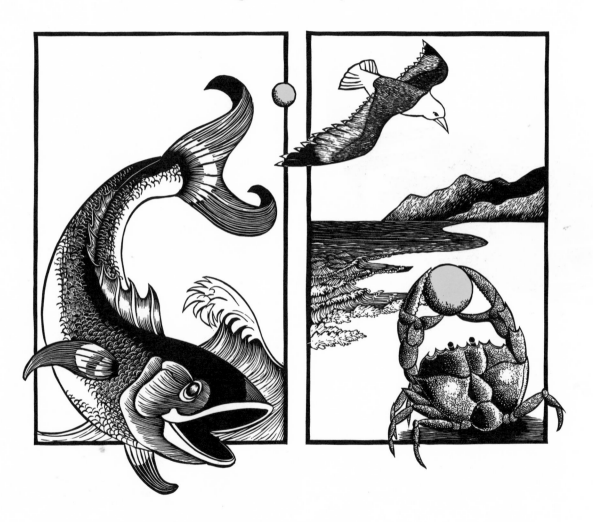

And two days later the tide brought it in.   But then . . .

I threw my yellow ball so far,

it struck a star.

The little star fell, so I made a wish on it. I wished

my yellow ball would fall all the way back down to earth

and a puppy would bring it home to me.

I closed my eyes,

and when I opened them,

there was the puppy with my yellow ball!   Then...

I threw my yellow ball nice and easy—

so the puppy could fetch it.

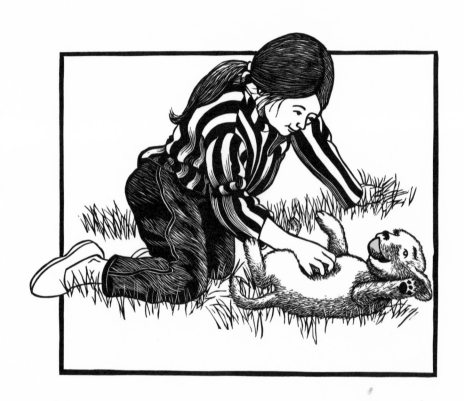

And she did.